The
Pup Who Cried
Wolf

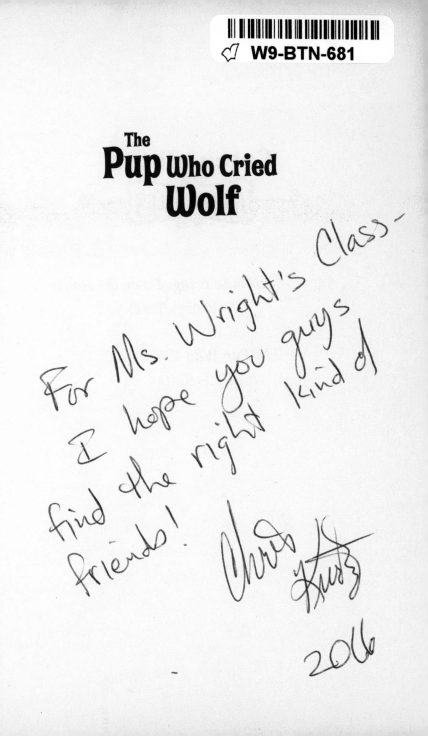

For Ms. Wright's Class—
I hope you guys
find the right kind of
friends!

Chris Kurtz

2016

Catch all the

ANiMAL TALES

Angus MacMouse Brings Down the House
Linda Phillips Teitel

The Pup Who Cried Wolf
Chris Kurtz

The
Pup Who Cried
Wolf

Chris Kurtz

illustrations by Guy Francis

BLOOMSBURY

NEW YORK BERLIN LONDON

For Janie,
whose words of wisdom can cut through my
most frenzied barking

First published in the United States of America in May 2010
by Bloomsbury Books for Young Readers
www.bloomsburykids.com

For information about permission to reproduce selections from this book, write to
Permissions, Bloomsbury BFYR, 175 Fifth Avenue, New York, New York 10010

Library of Congress Cataloging-in-Publication Data
Kurtz, Chris
The pup who cried wolf / by Chris Kurtz; illustrations by Guy Francis. — 1st U.S. ed.
p.   cm.
Summary: Lobo, a Chihuahua from New York City who feels he is truly a wolf in an
undersized body, goes to Yellowstone National Park with his mistress and
dreams of running wild with his wolf brothers.
ISBN 978-1-59990-492-4 (paperback) • ISBN 978-1-59990-497-9 (hardcover)
[1. Chihuahua (Dog breed)—Fiction.   2. Dogs—Fiction.   3. Yellowstone National
Park—Fiction.   4. Humorous stories.]   I. Francis, Guy, ill.   II. Title.
PZ7.K9626Pu 2010   [Fic]—dc22   2009038270

Book design by Danielle Delaney
Typeset by Westchester Book Composition
Printed in the U.S.A. by Worldcolor Fairfield, Pennsylvania
2 4 6 8 10 9 7 5 3 1 (paperback)
2 4 6 8 10 9 7 5 3 1 (hardcover)

All papers used by Bloomsbury Publishing, Inc., are natural, recyclable products
made from wood grown in well-managed forests. The manufacturing processes
conform to the environmental regulations of the country of origin.

Contents

1. Don't Mess with the Chihuahua 1

2. Brother Wolf on My Doorstep 9

3. Good News! 17

4. Top Predator Training for Speed 23

5. On the Trail. 30

6. Top Predator Training for Distance 39

7. The Call of the Pizza 44

8. Into the Heart of Wolf Country 48

9. Loving Lobo 55

10. Lobo, Was That You? 64

11. Even Top Predators Have to Say Sorry
    Sometimes 73

12. Freedom! 84

13. My Destiny 93

14. A Life-and-Death Matter 99

15. The Hunt 105

16. Brother Rat 110

17. Crazy Bird 115

18. A Glorious Escape 119

19. My Pack 128

Don't Mess with the Chihuahua

I've been waiting for a sign—a sign from my wild brothers that it's time to join their pack. Today could be the day. Just as yesterday could have been the day . . . but wasn't.

So far today has been pretty normal. But Mona is getting ready to take me to the park. Mona the beautiful. Mona the wonderful. Mona the one who wrapped me in a soft blanket when I was just a little thing.

I'm not little any longer. I'm a predator. A big, tough predator. Okay, I'm not that big. Actually, a little undersized, maybe. But that could be an advantage. Think of me as a dangerous wolf in a compact size.

That's why Mona never goes to the park without me.

Protection.

When we leave the safety of the apartment, I set the tone early. Do my job. Make a statement. Create a don't-mess-with-the-bad-boy-Chihuahua-or-the-beautiful-wonderfulness-in-the-flowing-skirt-and-loopy-earrings zone. Before I even step onto the sidewalk, I make up my mind to do my rapid-fire bark at the first person I see. Deep breath, dig down, let 'er rip! Bark, bark, bark. Ulp.

It turns out my target is an old lady pulling a wire cart on two wheels loaded with a large paper bag. Oops. Still, you never know what might be in a paper bag. Mona gets down to my level and scolds me. She seems to think the old lady is harmless and the bag contains groceries.

Mona is nice to everyone. Too nice. But deep down she understands she needs someone with a little grit to keep up the defenses.

Mona apologizes to the old lady while I peek in the bag. Groceries. Don't know how Mona guessed. But anybody can get lucky. Onions, three bananas, a loaf of bread, and . . . what's this? Tucked down under the bananas, three cans of Tabby Tidbits—Chicken à la King. A cat lover disguised as an innocent neighbor!

I give that woman another bark to let her know I have her little game figured out. Ulp. Mona tugs me down the street before I can warn the neighborhood.

Next we pass a couple of nasty cats on a windowsill, just sitting there because no one has the guts to make them move out. This is why neighbors with cat food are so dangerous. "Is that a squirrel on a leash?" says one cat.

Very funny. Luckily, I'm loaded with self-control. I decide to ignore them.

The other one laughs like this is the funniest thing she's ever heard. "Eat lots of acorns so you can grow up big and strong."

That does it. I bark and growl and lunge at them. Go right for the jugular. They're too dumb to even flinch. Just keep on laughing. Hrmpf!

Leashes. It's possible they can tell I'm attached to a rope.

"Lobo, mind your manners." Mona doesn't like me barking at the cats in the neighborhood, even when they start it. I bet she wouldn't mind so much if she could understand what they say.

All the way to the park, I remind myself about how excellent it is to be a dog with wolflike qualities. Cats! All they can dream about is that they come from . . . gee, let me see now . . . a cat! Wowee! My great-great-great-grandparents? Tough, beautiful wolves!

Finally we're at the park. There is no feeling in the world like the one you get when the leash comes off and you can run full tilt as far as you want. Of course, I don't stray too far from Mona. Like I said, she needs me.

Protection.

❧

When we get back to the apartment, Hector, the rat, has been busy. He has his brand-new cardboard-tube home chewed all the way to the ground. "Still sharp, still breaking it all down to size." He shows me his teeth. They are yellow and scary looking.

"That was your house," I say.

"Rats don't need houses," he says. "They need holes."

"I need a pack," I say. "Someday I'm going to find my wolf brothers."

"You could be my rat brother," he says. "We're almost the same size."

I would not be very excited about being a rat brother, but I don't say anything.

Suddenly, his nose goes up in the air. "Falafel."

"Huh?"

"Falafel. Extra hummus, extra onions." His nose twitches. "Extra yogurt."

I test the air. The rat is right. There is something delicious out there. But a rat sniffer hasn't been invented that can go up against a dog's nose. I sniff again. "Burrito," I say. "Beans, not hummus. That's a burrito."

"Falafel," says Hector. He's not giving up. And he sounds confident. A small tickle of doubt creeps into my mind. I can smell the spice, now. And is that . . . yogurt?

"Okay, okay. You nailed it." That hurts.

"Rat nose one, dog nose zero." Hector wiggles his behind to celebrate.

I hate losing our Next Top Smell game to a rat, and I especially hate losing to a showboating rat.

"Game's not over," I say. "Best two out of three. Next Top Smell." We both test the air.

"You first." Hector is looking cocky.

I catch the second scent immediately. "Cajun," I say. "Cajun chicken with black-eyed peas."

"Chicken yes, Cajun no." His little rat nose drifts from side to side. "Chinese. Pan fried . . ." He stops. "No, wait. That's not Chinese."

I can't keep from jumping up and doing a little side-step dance. "I knew it," I crow. "Someone's cooking Cajun down the hall." Mona brought Cajun home last week, and I never forget a smell.

"You got me, partner. Score is tied one to one." He smooths his whiskers. "Nice celebration dance, by the way."

"Thanks," I say. "Nice tail wiggle back there. Bump me."

We bump knuckles through the bars of his cage, finish up Next Top Smell, and I settle in for my morning nap.

Nothing has changed yet. No sign. But I still have a feeling today's the day.

Brother Wolf on My Doorstep

I'm in the middle of a beautiful dream when something hits my nose and wakes me up. There is a wood chip on the floor. Hector is staring at me. "What's your problem?" I say.

"You were having a nightmare," he says.

"No I wasn't. I was having a nice dream," I tell him.

"Well, you were twitching," he says, "and you look dumb when you twitch."

"All dogs twitch when they dream, Heckles." I call him Heckles when he annoys me . . . which is a lot. "It's a quality we inherited from our wolf ancestors, and it shows how alert we are, even during sleep."

"It looks weird," he says. "It looks weird on all dogs, but really weird on Chihuahuas."

He says this to make me mad. Hector is only a rat and he should be afraid of me. Some creatures—pet rats for instance—have had the wild bred right out of them, and they don't even know when to be afraid. I'm about ready to figure out how to open his cage and bite some wild into his fat rat behind when my extrasensitive ears hear a sound.

It's a special sound, a sign. I wait and it comes again.

This time I know for sure what it is, and I shiver with excitement. A wild lonely howl right in the middle of the city!

I jump up on the couch and run back and forth. "That was a wolf!" I say.

"Somebody save me!" says Hector in a high, fake voice. "A wolf has invaded New York City!"

I ignore his comedy routine and listen with my entire wolflike focus.

"*Que problema*," Glory squawks. I jump. I didn't know she was listening. Glory is a parrot from South America, and she tries to confuse people with her Spanish. "A wolf in the heart of New York City," she says. "Let's try and think if that is really possible."

She's almost always on my side. "Don't worry, Glory," I say. "If brother wolf comes around here, I'll stand between you and him and tell him old birds aren't very tasty."

"*Que bueno*," she says. "My protector. My warrior. And thanks so much for the compliment. I just love being thought of as an old bird."

"You're welcome," I say. *Que bueno* means "that's great." Glory has no idea I can understand almost everything she says in Spanish.

Glory got captured in the Amazon rain forest when she was a young bird and struggled against her cage night and day. But she doesn't mind the quiet life now. "This cage has everything I need," she says all the time. "Just right for a civilized parrot."

Mona always leaves the cage door open, and Glory hardly ever even steps out.

"Unfortunately," I say a little louder, "I won't be able to save everyone. If you are covered in white fur and have a naked tail, it's like wearing a sign that says EXTRA JUICY, and even a warrior cannot keep you safe from the wolf attack."

"If big brother wolf decides to come up and say hi to us city folk," says Hector, "remind me to ask him how his city brother can fit so many annoying habits into such a small package."

I lift one corner of my lip to show Hector my teeth.

The wolf howls again. I spin in a quick circle to locate the direction.

"Now, Lobo," Glory says. "I can see how you could mistake that sound. But I suspect there have been no wolves in this city since Manhattan was cleared of timber a couple of hundred years ago. I would say that the howl in question is more likely a garbage truck with bad brakes."

I listen. It's no secret that dogs have better hearing than either rats or parrots. Garbage truck! Ha! This wolf is one sly fellow. That's the thing about wolves, the secret for their incredible hunting success. They show up where you least expect them.

"If he calls again, I'm going to answer," I say. "Wolves like their brothers to answer when they call. Then they come a-running."

"Do wolves climb up the fire escape, or do they prefer the elevator?" asks Hector.

"Hey, bucktooth," I say. "Never underestimate a wolf. They are the most intelligent, crafty predators on the planet. And someday, if I get the chance, I may go hunting with them."

"Milk bones," says Heckles.

"What?" I say.

"Make sure that you tell your wolf

buddies that you want to go hunting for milk bones, because anything bigger or faster than a cookie in the shape of a bone is going to kick your tail."

Now I'm mad. I bark very loudly and very ferociously at Heckles.

He flattens himself against the wire of his cage. "Please don't hurt me, oh wild thing," he says. I can tell he isn't really afraid.

"Come to think of it, maybe you do have a wild brother," says Hector.

Finally. I thought I would never get through.

"Wolves have fleas. Wild fleas. Congratulations. You could be the brother of a wolf's wild flea."

I hear a sound like a parrot choking. Or trying not to laugh.

Sometimes when Glory should be sticking up for me, she doesn't remember.

"Watch it, Heckles." I walk over to him. "Someday the door of that cage might come unlatched and you'll have to face these." I show Hector my teeth.

"If this cage ever comes open, I'll march out

and bite the 'Chi' right off your 'huahua' before you can even turn around." Hector shows me his really scary yellow biters. I look away. To tell you the truth, they could give a dog nightmares, and even though I don't know what it is, I'm pretty sure I don't want to lose my "Chi."

Glory interrupts my thoughts. "Lobo, let's consider this. Don't wolves hunt at night?"

Glory asks hard questions sometimes, and when I'm worried or confused, I start licking. That tongue gets going, and I want to stop, but I can't.

Right now, my tongue is doing its thing. Toes. Back leg. Tummy. All I can think about is why I had the bad luck to be born in a city where wolves hardly ever go.

Just then a garbage truck revs its engine outside, and I can hear it driving to the next pickup. "Run for your life. Flea brother was right," says Hector. "Do wolves have four wheels, eat garbage one can at a time, and howl at streetlamps?"

Ha, ha, ha. I walk away, but I turn around just before I reach the corner. I look the dumb rat right in the eye. "That howling sound, my friend, is what is known as a sign! It's a sign that I'm going to find my pack someday, and that's a promise."

Wow. I can't believe I got a sign. Now I've got to stay on the lookout for the next sign. And then another sign and another. And then someday, a wolf.

Good News!

Mona is yakking on the phone in the kitchen. I'm hungry, and she's between me and my food. I try to scoot by. That doesn't work out.

"Come here, big boy." Wolves love being called big boy. So do wolf brothers. Is she in a scratching mood? She holds the phone to her ear with her shoulder and picks me up so we're face-to-face. Meanwhile, my legs dangle over the floor. Wolves hate dangling legs. So do wolf brothers.

Then she starts yakking to her mother again. Dogs have sensitive ears, as I said before, just like wolves. And none of us likes getting yakked over.

Without any warning, in between yaks, she kisses me on the nose. Of all the things wolves hate most, it's nose kissing. It's embarrassing. Wolf brothers aren't too crazy about it either.

Quickly, I slide an extra dollop of drool on my tongue and wait for the next nose kiss, because nose kisses never come in singles. *Sluuuurp.* I hit the bull's-eye on the second kiss.

"Ewww!" She puts me down pretty fast. I scamper to my food bowl. She might remember that lick next time she wants to yak in my ear and dangle my legs and give me nose kisses. You can train people if you have the know-how.

"You're a bad, bad dog!" she says to me. But she's laughing and telling her mother all about it while she wipes off the slobber.

Before I can get a bite of food, I hear an awful squawk. Glory is in trouble! I know just who the attacker is. Heckles! His mind must have snapped from grouchiness. He's finally figured a way to open that cage of his and is chasing her with his big yellow teeth.

Glory is very important to me. When I was a lonely little puppy, whimpering in the night, she was there for me, a voice in the darkness—a parrot voice, telling me that everything would be all right. And when that wasn't enough, there were songs and stories.

Now she's in trouble. Heckles might be chewing off Glory's "Chi" right now. If she has one.

I rush back for the rescue, woofing and howling. Actually, I'm still working on my woofing and howling. It might come out more like yipping and yapping. But it can still strike fear in the heart of the bravest scoundrel.

"Hey, Lobo," Mona yells, "quiet!" This makes me woof—okay, yap—even louder. If she knew what was happening to Glory, she would be depending on me to save her.

I can see it in my mind. Feathers everywhere. Glory being dragged to her doom. I dash up to the evil one's cage. I will scare him off just in case Glory is still clinging to life.

Then I see something that stops me short.

No feathers. No blood. Heckles is making a tunnel under his sawdust.

I look up.

Glory has her head cocked to one side, and one of her eyes is staring down at me in a confused sort of way.

I bark louder.

"Lobo, what is your problem?" Mona sticks her head around the corner. She's still on the phone.

My problem is that I am trying to do my job and maintain security and keep her beloved parrot from becoming rat chow. Except it turns out to be a false alarm because someone is playing with me. I glare at Glory and give another yip.

"Lobo, behave yourself." Mona stomps on the floor and uses that really scary voice that top predators hate.

I yelp. I admit it isn't the bravest of yelps in the world, but a lot of critters with less heart would tuck tail, scuttle underneath the sofa, and tremble. Not me. I have the heart of a wolf and I don't ever forget it. I tuck tail and scuttle underneath the sofa where I can watch for danger. My body is only shaking because the air-conditioning is making me cold.

Heckles pops his head out of his tunnel and

20

sniggers. A snigger is not a sound wolf brothers like to hear. I consider baring my battle weapons, my deadly fangs. But then I remember the scary voice and decide against it.

"What was that all about?" asks Glory.

I poke my ears out. "You squawked. I was ready to rescue you from danger."

"I am not in any danger," says Glory.

"So why the cry of fear and desperation?" I am determined to get to the bottom of this. "Perhaps I should tell you a story of a boy, or in this case a parrot, who cried wolf."

"My calling to you does not mean bark your head off and make a fool of yourself," says Glory, "and anyway, I am the one who told you that story when you were just a puppy."

"Oh," I say.

"It was a get-your-tail-in-here-and-pay-attention squawk. I was calling you because I heard something interesting while I was listening to Mona's conversation."

"What did she say?"

"She said..." Glory paused and preened. "Perhaps I shouldn't tell you. It could give you ideas. You could get in trouble if you don't think before you charge ahead."

Now I'm curious. I sit very quietly and politely to demonstrate just how thoughtful I really am.

"That was her sister on the phone. We're going to Yellowstone Park for the family reunion this year!"

Knock me over with a feather! I knew it! It's my next sign!

I leap up and run in a circle ten times. Glory knows Yellowstone Park means just one thing to me.

Wolves!

Top Predator Training for Speed

I wake up the next morning with a soaring heart. We are going camping. I have to get in shape to become a top predator.

And run with the wolves.

The lazybones of the world are still asleep. It's the perfect time for my first serious training exercise. Yellowstone might be wolf heaven, but it's no poodle party. There will be mountains to climb, rivers to cross, wide-open land to explore, and miles to run.

Chances like this don't come around more than once.

Ever since I heard the news, I've been planning out a special track to help me get ready. It's time to test it.

Mark. Set. Go! I race through the kitchen, streak under the dining room table, and leap up onto the coffee table.

Unfortunately, there is a pile of newspapers, a half can of soda, and a bowl of popcorn on the table. Using my wild instincts, I land on my feet as the newspapers slide off the table. Bang! The bowl of popcorn hits the floor.

White, buttery shapes fly around my head. I duck. I sidestep the rolling can with soda pouring out, and bound forward before the last kernel of popcorn stops bouncing.

Hah! Back around the track. Let me tell you, it's not easy taking corners on a hardwood floor. Dog feet aren't made to stick on smooth wood, so mostly they slide. I take at least five extra running steps on every turn.

Dog claws don't help much either. Mostly dog claws make running a lot louder.

Suddenly a fluffy yellow and pink bedroom

slipper in the shape of a fish comes flying out of nowhere. It just misses my ear.

Red alert! Prowlers have gained entry and are trying to take out the guard dog with a shoe gun. My instincts switch from training mode to watchdog mode. I bark. I stop and spin around to spot the intruder.

Dear, sweet Mona is standing in the hall just outside the bedroom door. The bandits must have awakened her. She looks terrible. Her hair is sticking out everywhere. She looks like she could use another two hours of sleep. And she has her arm cocked back with a weapon in her hand. It is a fluffy yellow and pink fish in the shape of a slipper.

She has the same weapon as the intruders! What a confusing coincidence. I decide to ignore the confusion and focus on the job at hand.

I bark again and do a 360 to keep the enemy pinned down.

Mona must have the same idea. A second slipper comes whizzing through the air. No, not whizzing exactly. Fluffy bedroom slippers don't whiz so much as they flutter. The problem is, it's hard to aim a slipper, and instead of hitting the intruder it hits me. Right in the ribs.

I yelp to let her know that she missed her target, but she disappears into the bathroom.

She must think I've already scared off the bad guys. I sniff around just to make sure, and try not to step in the sticky mess of soda and popcorn. All clear. That was a close one.

"Nice work, Wolfie."

I turn around. Heckles is yawning and rubbing his whiskers sleepily.

"You're just lucky you're worthless," I tell the rat. "Otherwise, you could have been stolen. A burglar was just in here. A sneaky burglar who thought he could get past the defenses of a wolf brother and not be detected."

"Burglar." He snorts.

"Mona's lucky I'm around," I say. "That burglar

could have cleaned her out. I wonder how he got away so fast."

I think about taking another exercise lap or two around the apartment, but I decide against it. I need to be rested and alert in case the intruder comes back.

I head to the kitchen, where a bright red bowl with white paw prints all around the sides is waiting. Running laps and chasing out intruders has made me hungry. I hope I didn't eat all of my Nibbles and Nuggets The Simple Formula for the Super Dog from last night.

Nibbles and Nuggets, for short, are yummy. Each nugget is a perfect circle, exactly the same as every other nugget, and each nibble is a tasty triangle. Duck-flavored and delicious.

Sure enough, I am still munching, trying to keep my energy up, when Mona comes in.

She looks at me and crosses her arms. I can tell she is still grumpy about the burglar. Me, I'm already over it, and I'm the one who got smacked in the ribs for my trouble.

That gives me an idea. I gulp down my last bite and then try to take a step. Oh, no! My left hind leg is all injured and limpy. Head down. Tail between my legs. I limp away from her. Sad, sad eyes. Limp, limp, limp. Go right for the heart. Every dog knows how to do this. Stop, turn, and look. Betrayed. Abused. Then limp some more.

It's working! She comes over and scratches behind my ears. Ohhh, that feels good. Her hand runs down my spine. Ahhh. Then ever-so-gently she checks out my poor limpy leg.

I flinch. Then I start trembling to make sure she feels good and sorry. I'm listening for the magic words that will definitely make my leg feel a lot better.

"Do you need to go outside?"

Wahoo! The most magic words of all! I bark and turn in circles.

Oops. *Hurt leg. Limp some more.* It's possible to recover a little too quickly from these things. The trick with humans is to get them to do what you want, and still let them think they are in charge.

After she gets dressed and cleans up the mess, she checks me over a couple more times to make sure I'm all right before we go for our morning walk. I love our morning walks! Not that I need them, you understand. A wolf doesn't need anything other than a full moon once a month, and a pack to go hunting with.

Soon I'll be part of the pack. My training plan will turn me into a strong, trim hunting machine.

I make myself a promise that I'll do anything I can to grab this chance.

On the Trail

The entire week, Mona packs for Yellowstone. Honestly, I don't understand why anyone needs so much stuff. I say, just grab the dog food and let's go.

Finally, the big day arrives. I sit on the front seat of the car knowing we are heading for the best place on earth for a wolf brother.

Yellowstone Park is wolf heaven. Summer nights are warm and perfect for the hunt. After the howls go up, the pack becomes silent and moves through the trees like shadows. Small animals burrow into their holes or scamper up into the branches. But the pack takes no notice. The wolves seek larger prey. I wonder if elk or deer will be on the menu the first night.

In the winter, the bears sleep in their caves and snow covers the land. Bison gather in groups for warmth. But not the wolves. Cold does not bother them. On the ground, the animal tracks lead the way, and the wolf pack is on the move once again.

Now I'm on the move too.

Dogs love road trips. We are delightful traveling companions. It's a quality that sets us above many other animals. Hippos come to mind, for instance. You hardly ever hear about hippos on road trips, and I've heard it's because the minute you get on the freeway, they need to go to the bathroom. When you ask why they didn't go before you left, they say they didn't need to before but now they do.

Dogs take exactly the right number of potty breaks.

Think about it. Would you rather go on a trip with a dog or a spitting cobra? A dog or a cricket? A dog or a slug? Everyone knows that spitting cobras get grouchy after the first twelve miles, and after that they just lie there and stare at you without blinking.

Crickets sing the same song over and over, and just when you think you are going to lose your mind, they sing it again.

Slugs are easygoing and they don't ask for much. Everything might look just fine until you decide you'd like some conversation. You can ask a slug questions all morning long and not get an answer.

While we're on the subject, you might add rats and parrots to your list. Parrots get carsick. They moan and sway inside their cages.

As for rats . . . well, they just act like rats.

Lucky for Mona, she has a dog. Having a good trip is obviously all up to me.

Mona's car is a hot little sporty thing. It's one of her best features. You can put your front feet up on the armrest and hang your head out of the window even if you're small.

Not that I'm small. A little undersized, maybe. Which could be a good thing.

On the freeway I hang my head out of the

window. The wind whips my ears back. I bark at anyone who gets too close, one lane away or so. Maybe two. Just in case they get any funny ideas of bothering me or Mona. Mona tells me to pipe down.

Pipe down, indeed. She should tell the parrot, moaning and groaning under the towel over her cage, to pipe down.

Mona doesn't understand about all the dangers out there. It's like a sixth sense for me, and poor Mona just doesn't have it. But I pipe down to be polite—and so she doesn't roll up the window. Driving with the window down and your head in the wind is like being on a hunt. The smells come by so fast, you need a wolf's powerful mind to sort it all out. Which, lucky for me, I have. Being a wolf brother is a big advantage.

Unfortunately, if you're not careful, a big whoosh of wind can plow right up your nose when you don't expect it. Wind going that fast can rearrange things up in there. That's what happens to me. I have to sneeze about five times to get my nose back to normal.

Mona seems to think that I'm spraying dog spit all over the car. I don't think it's such a big deal, but up goes the window.

Heckles sniggers. With my sharp hearing, I detect it even though he's in the backseat.

I don't know why Mona hasn't learned that you should never, EVER take a rat on a road trip. They cause multiple problems. But Mona says she won't go anywhere without her family.

I sigh. I press my nose against the window.

If there was ever a time to feel sorry for myself, this is it.

Why should Heckles even get to be part of the family? He can't stop moving around in his cage. He gets sawdust all over the backseat. He poops inside the car whenever he feels like it with no regard for others. And he sniggers.

It's about time for a good pout. Even good traveling companions need to have a good pout now and then to make a point. I tuck my tail and drop down to the floor. It takes experience and skill to be a good pouter. Slump down with a sigh. Head on paws. Little whimpers. But most of all, sad, sad eyes.

Mona has no defense against the pout. She stops the car and lifts me back on the seat. She says she's glad to have such a strong, tough watchdog that never lets anything get by him.

The window doesn't go back down, though, so I keep my pouty face right where it is.

She starts in with the fingers.

Oh, the fingers! First she rubs my head. Then she tickles my ears. Then I roll over and she starts on my tummy. If I get lucky, she'll find the just-can't-help-myself spot. The just-can't-help-myself spot makes a dog's back leg go nuts.

It's like a tummy party. It feels so good that the leg on the scratching side wants to join in. It just goes around and around like a windup leg until the party is over. Oooh, there it is. Mona finds the just-can't-help-myself spot, and pretty soon there's no more pout left in me. I look around for something to do.

"*Psst*, Heckles." I jump into the backseat. "I'm bored. Wake up."

Hector opens his eyes, and I can tell he hasn't really been asleep. "I don't feel so good."

"Let's play Next Top Smell," I say.

"You go first," he says. He can't resist the chance to beat me at Next Top Smell.

I sniff. "Top Smell. Hmmm." I sniff again. "Rat pee."

"Duh," says Hector. "What do you want me to do, hold it all the way to Yellowstone?"

"You don't even hold it around the block," I say. "Okay, your turn. Second to the Top Smell."

Hector sniffs. "Second to Top Smell . . . air freshener. Pine tree–type."

"Double duh," I say. "Been smelling that thing before we got out of the parking garage." I look at the little cardboard tree hanging from the rearview mirror. This isn't working out so great.

"I got an idea," says Hector. "Let's play go back to sleep." He curls into a ball.

Sleep doesn't sound like such a bad idea. Sleep builds bones. It's good for toughening me up to prepare for life with the pack. Anyway, there's nothing else to do now that the window is rolled up.

I hop back up and circle round and around on the front seat. I follow my tail for two and a half turns. Then I settle down and tuck my nose in for a long ride.

I wait for my mind to go far away to my wild place. That place isn't so far away any longer. It's getting closer with every turn of the tires.

In my wild place, the wind blows across the long buffalo grass. And something is crouching down, out of sight—hiding. The buffalo eating the buffalo grass don't suspect a thing.

The wolf leader has brought the pack around so that they are downwind. He is wise. He is experienced. He is a good leader even if he is a small fellow. Not too small. Just a little under-sized, maybe.

Which could be a good thing if you're hiding in the buffalo grass and sneaking up on a herd of buffalo.

Top Predator Training for Distance

Yellowstone is a long way from New York City. I have two or three bone-building snoozes in between rest breaks before Mona finally stops the car at a motel. After we get Hector and Glory and Mona's suitcase stashed away in the room, it's still light out. So Mona and I go off to find the nearest park in this small town.

I charge against the leash all the way to the park. I'm not going to miss a single opportunity to increase my strength. Mona yanks my leash back a hundred times, but I'm unstoppable. I bark and growl at all the cats. We meet up with a few dogs.

There is a ridiculous-looking pretty boy with long hair. Afghan hound, I think they call his breed. He tries to sniff me up under the tail, and I spin around on him so quick he bumps his little walnut brain against his paper skull.

The boxer and the yellow Lab we cross paths with get a taste of some serious practice—barking and growling. Their owners give Mona dirty looks, and they pass us on the other edge of the sidewalk. After that, Mona keeps me on a pretty short tether, which is too bad because we meet a puffy little white cutie, and I don't get a chance to even touch noses. I can tell she wanted to, though.

As soon as we arrive at the park, Mona unclips my leash and I begin some serious training. My extrasensitive nose picks up the scent of a wild creature. Possibly large. Possibly very dangerous. Possibly with a great big rack of horns, and giant hooves.

Who knows what kind of critters they let run around in these small-town parks? I'm thinking there could be a water buffalo loose in the park. Luckily I'm just the dog to handle the situation.

I finally track him down, and when he sees me on his trail, he jumps into the branches of an oak tree. It turns out to be a squirrel. What a trickster! I put the fear of dog into him for impersonating a buffalo. He won't be trying that again for a while.

Now that I've made sure the park is safe for Mona, it's time for my strength and endurance training. Everyone knows that wolves hunt by running their prey into the ground, and I'm determined to be in tip-top shape when I'm called on to lead the pack. Of course, I'll be respectful of the leader, but it won't take long for the pack to think maybe they should consider me for the job of top banana.

I gallop in a large circle around Mona. I figure fifteen laps will track down the most stubborn elk.

Five laps and I'm not one bit tired.

Seven laps and still running strong.

Seven and a half laps . . . whew!

I sink down in a heap. Time to refigure my calculations. Six laps' worth of running should be all I need to catch even the most stubborn elk. Mona

comes and picks me up. I snuggle into her arms and give her a grateful lick.

She says some very nice things to me. It seems she was very impressed. She carries me for a block or so on the way back to the motel. Even wolves in tip-top shape need some recovery time after a long, hard run.

The Call of the Pizza

Back at the motel, as soon as Mona steps into the shower, Glory starts complaining. "I can't understand why people want to go camping." She fluffs up her feathers. "Somebody tell me why you would go and build a nice big city with air-conditioning and bright lights and flavors from all over the world, and then choose to drive thousands of miles to sleep on the ground and have pine needles in your oatmeal."

"It's the call of the wild," I tell her. "Of all the creatures that live in this family, you should understand the best. You're the only one who has ever been wild."

"What about the call of the pizza? What about the call of the warm bed?" Glory steps up on the top bar of her cage and swings upside down, hanging by her toes. "Tell me what is so great about not knowing where your next meal is going to come from." She starts swinging back and forth, still upside down. "And tell me what's so great about shivering in the cold and worrying about who is trying to eat you."

"One word," Hector says. "Freedom."

He is sniffing at the wire corners of his cage. Freedom. Life outside the walls. Hector wants it just as bad as I do. He says he's a wild rat in his bones, and if he ever gets out, he is going to live underground and procreate.

He thinks I don't know what that means. I do. It means he's going to make lots of babies with a girl rat.

"Freedom," I echo. "The kind wolves have."

"You're obsessed with wolves," says Hector.

"At least I'm not obsessed with girls," I tell him.

"Gentlemen, no fighting," says Glory. "Don't

act like backyard mutts and barn-raised vermin. Anyway, you don't know what you're talking about."

Glory swings herself back right side up and turns to face us. "What's wrong with protection? What's wrong with style? Have you thought about teeth and claws and animals looking at you like you are a walking chicken nugget? *Que loco.* You two crazy birds go ahead and get back to your roots. Just don't call me when your stomach starts grumbling and winter is just around the corner."

Glory turns her back and starts whistling to show that the conversation is over.

"What was that all about?" I say to Hector.

"How sad." Hector shakes his head. "All the wild has been drained out of her system." He fluffs himself up and walks around his cage on two feet. "What about teeth and claws and yackety-yackety-yak!" It's a perfect imitation.

That night, Mona and I cuddle on the motel bed and look at photo albums. There's the mountain lake from last year's family reunion. Nice, but no Yellowstone Park! There's Mona's dad and his motor home where we slept. There's Mona's sister.

And there ... I wince. Under all the grime, it's a little girl, perhaps. Red hair. A smile that's too big for the face. And what is that in her arms? A doll in a frilly pink dress with a dog's head? A small dog's head? Actually, not too small ... it's me!

Alexandra. Mona's niece. She's a fearsome little thing that even a wolf would want to stay far away from.

I let my head sink down on my paws. Maybe she won't be there this time.

Yellowstone isn't a big attraction for some kids. She might be staying with friends. Or her friends might come too, and she'll be too busy playing with them and won't have time to dress up her auntie's Chihuahua in doll clothes. Or she might be too old for dolls any longer. But probably she won't even be there.

Yes. Almost definitely she won't be there. I decide not to worry about it. Even Alexandra can't ruin my mood for long.

8

Into the Heart of Wolf Country

Anyone with a good nose and a wild heart can feel the change. I know it the moment we cross the line. Wilderness. I can feel it in my teeth.

Also it helps that there is a big wooden sign that says YELLOWSTONE NATIONAL PARK, and a Yellowstone National Park ranger station with a sign that says YELLOWSTONE NATIONAL PARK RANGER STATION. And the other thing that helps me figure out where we are is the ranger who comes out to the car and says, "Welcome to Yellowstone National Park."

The ranger sounds all friendly, but he turns out to be a rude sort. "Oh, a killer dog," he says when he sees me. He tells Mona to keep the windows up as soon as we leave the ranger station. He probably knows I'll hate that. He says don't feed the bears. Then he mentions some silly law. "Keep your dog on a leash at all times inside the park."

Umm, how am I going to meet my wolf pack on a leash?

"Usually we say that to protect the smaller wildlife such as squirrels." The ranger is still talking. "But in his case, the squirrels might just mistake him for one of their babies that fell out of the tree, carry him back upstairs, and stuff him full of nuts."

Ha, ha, ha. Oh boy. I am so done with this guy. I give him a taste of my rapid-fire barking to show what I think of him.

"Keep the noise down," he says. "Otherwise, I'll have to get out my flyswatter."

Mona starts laughing, and Glory, who has been quiet up till now, starts giggling. And then I hear a snigger. Heckles. That's it. I'm finished with this family and ready to find my pack.

Somehow.

Someway.

Leash or no leash, I am going to escape.

The ranger obviously likes being Mr. Funny, and he leans down to talk a little longer to Mona.

"Keep an extra close watch on him. We've got mosquitoes in the park that could carry him off and feed him to their young." I turn my back on the ranger. He probably has a shriveled-up heart from living so close to the wilderness and not being a brother to anything wild at all. I drop to the floor and slump down with my head on my paws. We'll just see how my fellow travelers like having the best traveler in the bunch go on a major pout.

The problem is, when we get moving again, I want to smell everything. I hop back up on the seat. It's not easy pouting when you're this excited. Unfortunately, Mona has listened to the ranger and is carefully following the rules. The only air is coming through Mona's air-conditioning system. I start whining and whimpering.

That doesn't get the window to come down, so I put my slobber setting on high and go to work licking the windows. That almost always works, but not today. Today all I get is Mona telling me she's going to stick me in the backseat. That gets my tongue back in my mouth pretty quick. There is a powerful odor of rat pee coming from back there, and it isn't getting any fresher with the windows rolled up.

We drive slowly, and pretty much the only thing to see is the big butt of the motor home crawling along ahead of us. Finally we turn into a campsite. I start whining and slobbering again. I can't help it, I'm so excited.

"There's Mom and Dad's motor home," Mona says. "And oh look, there's little Alexandra."

I stop slobbering. I stop whining. I stop breathing.

No! It can't be. How could her parents let her come to a wild place like this?

Alexandra is not hard to spot. Just look for the critter with more energy than a gerbil on an exercise wheel and more freckles than common sense. We see her before she sees us, which is a good thing. I drop down out of sight.

"You're so lucky." Mona reaches over and

scratches my ears. "She loves animals extra-much."

Hector moans a little rat moan.

"*Que problema,*" says Glory from behind her towel. She and Hector and I have all had experience with Alexandra who loves animals extra-much. My last memory of the little darling was me hanging upside down, her grubby little hand holding me by my left hind leg.

"You three are in for a good time," says Mona. "No brothers or sisters. No pets allowed in her apartment, poor thing. She loves you guys!"

Less love. Please, less love! As we pull into the campsite, I peek over the windowsill. Poor thing jumps up and knocks over her chair. She shrieks and comes running with her pigtails flying. Alexandra looks just as wild as ever. In fact there is only one difference I can see from the last time I was dangled like a chew toy in her hands.

She's bigger.

"Prepare for the attack." I jump into the backseat. The passenger side door is ripped open before Mona can even stop the car.

"Did you bring Lobo?" Alexandra shrieks. She has a voice that could scramble an egg.

I scurry down to the floor to hide.

"Grab the dog," says Hector. "Please grab the cute little dog."

A freckly, nail-chewed hand reaches behind the chair and latches on to me.

"Oooh, he's so cute, Aunt Mona."

No amount of digging into the carpet helps.

"Be kind," says Mona.

Alexandra pulls.

"Be careful," says Mona.

Alexandra hauls. I'm being reeled in like a fish on a line. Backward.

"Alexandra, be gentle," says Mona.

I'm dragged out of my hiding spot. There's nothing kind or careful or gentle about this. I'm about to be hoisted into the air by my left hind leg.

"Alexandra, no!" Mona's voice reminds me of my puppy days, when I thought it might be fun to piddle on her shoe. But it's too late.

Being upside down is starting to feel very familiar.

Loving Lobo

Mona scrambles out of the car and dashes around to the other side. It is my secret dream to watch Alexandra get a swat on the hindquarters with Mona's appointment book. And then Mona might remind Alexandra that I am a dangerous creature with wild ancestors who can never be fully trusted around small children.

Instead, "I know you're not used to animals, sweetie," is all Mona says. "Here. Let me show you."

Mona's soothing hands get me right side up.

It's good of her to try, but "sweetie" has been up to these same tricks longer than I can remember. Glory tells stories about Alexandra that happened before Hector and I were even born. The minute Mona turns her back, I'm in trouble.

Now that I'm upright, I get hugged in the much-too-tight way.

"Easy, honey," says Mona.

Easy, honey? How about bad girl! Bad, bad girl. My ear is crushed against Alexandra's bony chest so hard I can hear the drumbeat of her heart.

"You have to be very, very kind to my little family." Mona reaches down and eases my position. "Okay, Alexandra? Promise?"

"Okay, Aunt Mona. I promise." Alexandra pats my head. "Sorry, Lobo."

"Now, you wait right here," Mona says, "and hold Lobo very gently while I say hello to everyone."

Uh-oh. Mona is turning away to get hugs from her mother and father and sister. Alexandra is not waiting right here. I have a bad feeling about this.

At least Alexandra is holding me gently now. But she takes me straight to her tent. I see a familiar box. A box filled with beads and scarves and ribbons and bows.

"Lobo." Alexandra gives me a mostly gentle hug. "You are going to be the best-looking one at the whole ball!"

Best-looking? This doesn't sound so bad.

"Aunt Mona, come play with me!" Alexandra hollers into my ear. "I'm the princess and Lobo wants to be my long-lost twin sister!"

I change my mind. Lobo does not want to go to the ball or be anyone's twin sister, and she ... he does not care any longer if he is the best looking. Fortunately, Mona understands the emergency and comes running.

Unfortunately, Mona does not put an end to the game but instead joins in. For a half hour that seems like forever, I am the lovely sister to Princess Alexandra. She ties strings of plastic pearls and leopard print scarves around my neck.

Mona spends most of her time saying things like, "Not too tight, honey." Or "Be gentle, angel." Or "Sweetheart, I don't think Lobo likes it when his dress gets tangled around his legs."

Let me tell you. Lobo does not like that at all!

Finally it is time to go to the ball. After being introduced to all the handsome princes, Alexandra picks up my front paws and we go dancing about. Mona giggles and keeps busy by following us and loosening the items around my neck that I can't help stepping on.

Finally the little monster's mother calls.

"Off you go, princess," Mona says to Alexandra. "It's supper time. You can finish loving Lobo later."

Oooh, so much to look forward to. Thanks, Mona.

Alexandra's little feet pad off to the table.

"Okay, twin sister," Mona says to me. She looks at me and giggles. "You haven't had so much attention since you were a puppy. You must love this."

Honestly, the ball, the dancing, the strings of pearls winding around my feet . . . not really my thing. Thank goodness Mona stayed close by. She manages to get my beautiful scarves removed, and I get a tummy party and a back scratch for my trouble. Things are looking up, and for a moment I think I might even get a little bit of leash-free exploration time.

Sadly, Mona has not forgotten the ranger's rules. She clips a chain to my collar just as I am making up my mind which way to run. The chain is attached to the bottom step of the large motor home, and Mona disappears before I even remember to pout.

My chain is long enough for me to hop up inside the motor home to find Hector and Glory, who are side by side in their cages on the floor.

"He's still alive," says Glory, giving me a slight wave with one wing, "and not much worse for the wear."

"Oooh, he's so cute!" says Hector in a high girl voice.

"And thank you for your support," I tell Hector. "With any luck it will be your turn after supper."

I throw myself down between Hector and Glory. Even though they aren't anything like a wolf family, it feels good to be back with these two.

Luck turns out to be on my side. In between supper and s'mores, Alexandra asks Mona to unhook the door to Hector's cage. She hauls him out by his tail, with Mona trying to show her how to be kind, and carries him away. In spite of myself, I feel just a tiny bit sorry for him.

"I'll be next," says Glory with a heavy sigh.

There's nothing I can say.

At bedtime, Alexandra comes stomping up the stairs of the motor home with Hector in her hands, complaining that she isn't even tired. She might not be, but I can tell that Hector is going to get a good night's sleep.

"Oh, my aching ears," he complains as he is dumped back into his cage. Mona latches the door behind him, and he hugs the wires with his little hands. "Home sweet home."

"We need a plan," I say.

"Exactly." Hector throws himself down in a corner. "You two make a plan while I sleep off the agony. I'm counting on you."

In another moment he is snoring. Glory and I look at each other. She doesn't look like she has any more ideas than me—and I have zero.

Then far out in the distance I hear something that makes the hairs on the back of my neck sit up and pay attention. It's the howl of a wolf. It is not the bad brakes on a garbage truck. It is not my imagination. It is a wolf and I can tell that Glory hears it too.

I start to shiver so hard from excitement that I can hardly get my next words out. "I'm p-p-pretty sure we could learn a thing or two about getting out of a tight spot from w-w-wolves."

"I'm afraid a wolf's set of skills will not help you right now," says Glory.

"How do you know? Have we tried slashing with fangs and going for the jugular?"

"I tried a bite or two when I was a younger bird," says Glory. "Trust me. Mona wants Alexandra to learn how to treat us well. But Alexandra is family for Mona. She does not want Alexandra harmed in the process."

I listen for more wolf calls, but the night is quiet except for crickets.

"If I was with the wolves, I wouldn't have these problems," I say.

"Wolves have problems," says Glory. "Do you think wild creatures have it easy?"

I don't answer Glory. But I know she has me figured out all wrong. Maybe some dogs are happy with the soft life. But not this dog.

Not a dog in the land of his ancestors.

Not a dog who is determined to find his pack even if he is a little on the small side.

Not small, exactly. A little undersized, maybe.

Mona comes in. She rubs my tummy, scratches Glory under her neck feathers just where she likes it, and wakes up Hector to give him a peanut. Then she goes to the back of the motor home to sleep.

It's quiet except for the night sounds. I let my mind fly away to the windswept hill where the howl came from. The wolves are howling and dancing around another, smaller wolflike guy. They are waiting for the signal only he can give.

Then the leader raises his head. His howl floats over the trees, and all the animals of the forest turn to listen.

Lobo, Was That You?

"Are you awake?" Two big, blue eyes in the middle of a small face and a tangle of uncombed hair are the first things I see in the early morning light. It scares me so much I almost pitch off the couch where I've made my bed. But I can't, because there are two hands around my middle.

"Stay right here with me and I'll rock you to sleep," Alexandra says.

Do I have a choice? She wraps me in a doll's blanket and holds me up to her shoulder and leans her head down until her bird's-nest hair covers my nose.

"Hush, baby," she says. "Mommy will wash all the nightmares out of your head." She starts to rock and hum. "Shhhh. You're safe with me."

Well, too bad we don't share the same opinion about that. I squirm to let her know I'd rather be free, but there is no letting up of her grip. Alexandra switches me over to the other shoulder and pats my back. "Do you need to burp?"

Umm. Thank you for asking, but no. This calls for action. I can always bark really loudly to get some attention from the adults. But I have a better idea. I whine.

I'm pretty sure none of the sleepyhead adults in the back rooms want to clean up Chihuahua piddle on their nice motor home rug because they waited too long to let the poor guy out.

I don't hear anything so I whine again. Sure enough, a puffy-eyed Mona appears at the door. "Alexandra?" She blinks a few times. "What are you doing?"

"Nothing."

I bark so that Mona knows that the nothing under the doll's blanket is me.

"Alexandra, why are you holding Lobo? Remember, you're supposed to wait for me before you hold him, so I can make sure you're being safe."

"I think Lobo was having a nightmare," says Alexandra.

Oh no he wasn't. Not until you decided to wake him up.

"Besides, I just love your family so much, Aunt Mona. It's hard for me not to hold them."

I struggle out of the doll's blanket and out of Alexandra's hands and land right at Mona's feet.

"I know you do, honey," says Mona, "but it's really early. Let's take Lobo outside for a potty break and then go back to bed for a while."

"Okay." Alexandra jumps up. "Aunt Mona, you're my favorite."

$\sim$

After breakfast and after two hours of hide-and-seek, kick the can, and freeze tag, favorite Aunt Mona looks dusty and tired. She decides to take a shower and then go for a sightseeing ride around the park. Alexandra says she wants to come too, but Mona tells her that she needs to have a little family time. I think Mona just needs to get away from Alexandra for a while.

Mona hums a tune while she packs. Glory makes bird sounds and swings upside down when her cage gets loaded in the backseat. Hector scratches his back on the wire sides of his cage and says, "Mmm, mmm," over and over. Everyone is in a good mood for a little family time . . . or could it be that we're all just glad to be escaping a certain someone?

On the road, Mona cracks the window for me even though it's against the rules. My feet go up on the armrest. Ahh, the wind in the ears. Ahh, the wild smells. I sniff. I breathe deeply. Ulp. I almost choke.

Glory stops twittering. Mona plugs her nose. "Lobo, was that you?"

I drop down to the seat and lick the sides of my mouth to try and wipe the taste off my tongue. I know what Mona is thinking, and I am shocked that she suspects me.

"Smells exactly like . . . air of dog," says Hector, "and I don't want to say which end it came from."

Glory giggles.

"It wasn't me," I say. It really wasn't. The problem is, no one believes me because that's the same thing I say when it really *is* me.

Mona keeps her nose plugged. "It's getting worse and it's coming from outside." She rolls up the windows. For once I'm glad.

"Ha." I turn to face Hector. "Told you it wasn't me."

The sign says BUBBLING PAINT POTS. Apparently, it's some "natural wonder" people like to see, because Mona stops to take a look. There are bubbles. But not like bath bubbles. These are mud bubbles that expand like brown balloons out of the ground and then pop and splatter mud in all directions. Hot, bubbling mud from the middle of the earth, and crowds of people. Everyone with any sense, and two fingers, is holding their nose.

Not an animal in sight . . . except for the poor critters on leashes like me who can't hold our noses. No animal would want to be anywhere near this place. Now, if you were a dirty sock, you would feel like you were in a heaven where all dirty socks end up. But this was no place for anyone with lungs. We hustle out of there.

"Let's go see a lake," says Mona. *Great*, I think. *Cool, fresh breezes. Children splashing on the shore.* Mona turns off the road and I get a bad feeling when I see the sign. SOUR LAKE. Swimming, anyone? No thanks. The next sign is worse. DANGER! BOILING WATER. UNSTABLE GROUND. And if that sign isn't enough to make you drive away, just look at all the trees around the edge of Sour Lake. Dead. And if the boiling water didn't kill the trees, I think it might have been the smell. Mona drives away.

I'm a lot happier when we are speeding away from the stink and out to the meadows of long grass. The window comes down again. Out here it smells like . . . I sniff again . . . grass. Weird.

And there's another smell. A wild smell.

My wolf senses go on high alert. "Something is out there," I say. I get so excited, my front feet start to prance on the armrest. I make them stop because I'm pretty sure wolves don't prance. "Something dangerous with sharp teeth." Only an animal with a howl in his heart can possibly know this. "Could be wolves!"

"Horns," says Hector.

Horns? How can he be so sure? I sniff again. "Claws," I say. "Definitely something with sharp, dangerous claws."

"Hooves," says Hector.

He sounds very sure of himself and I have a bad feeling about this. I might have let my excitement get ahead of my nose in this one case only. But I don't want to lose. I look back at Hector. He is stretching up as tall as his little rat self can stretch and sniffing like crazy.

Then I notice that with his cage sitting on the backseat, the windows are too high for him to see out.

I look ahead. "I'll let you know what it is when I see it."

Mona slows down. There *is* something in the meadow. Long thin legs. Horns. It is eating grass.

I'm pretty disappointed with myself, but I act confident. "Ooh, ouch," I say. "Nice try back there, mousie. It's a bear."

Hector starts sniffing like crazy. His nose is twitching, and he gets on his hind feet and goes from one end of his cage to the other trying to catch the scent. "Are you sure?" he asks.

"Big, brown, and bearish," I lie. "Teeth as long as scissors."

Hector gets back down on all fours and bangs his head against the wire of his cage. "I don't know what's wrong with me."

"Hey, look." Mona points. "There's a deer."

"A deer!" Hector stops banging and looks at me. His eyes squint. "You said it was a bear."

I look back out the window. "Oh that," I say. "Yeah, that's a deer. I was talking about the bear right . . . oops, it just stepped out of sight."

Hector stomps around his cage and then grabs the wire bars. "Bring your bony little leg over here," he growls. "I want to show you something."

I don't move. He bites the wires with his yellow teeth. I think I would rather face a bear than Hector right now. I look away.

A wood chip comes flying out of Hector's cage and zings me on the ear. I probably deserved that.

11

Even Top Predators Have to Say Sorry Sometimes

"Yellowstone's greatest prize is coming up!" Mona sounds excited.

I look back at Hector. He squints his eyes at me again and sticks out his tongue. Hector is still mad.

I jump to put my feet up on the armrest of the door so I can look out the window. I wag my tail. But inside, my tail is dragging. I know I'm the reason for Hector's bad mood, and for once I feel like it's my fault.

I jump into the backseat. "Hey, Heckles," I say. "There's a big attraction coming up."

Hector's tongue goes back in his mouth, but his eyes get even squintier. "That was not a cool move back there," he says.

"I don't know what you're talking about," I say. "I'm pretty sure there was a bear right behind the ..."

I look at Glory. She is staring at me and she shakes her head.

"Whatever," I say. "You're just a big grump."

I look out the window. From down here on the backseat where Hector has to stay, there isn't much to see. The tops of trees go floating past now and then, but it's mostly all clouds and sky. I look at Hector. He has his eyes closed but I don't think he's sleeping.

Mona pulls off the road. There is another sign. The big attraction turns out to be a geyser called Old Faithful. I have no idea what a geyser is. Mona pulls her car into the parking lot and stops near a tree. She's all in a rush, as if she's going to miss something if she doesn't hurry. She runs to find an open bench in the crowd and then comes back for us.

One by one she grabs Hector and then Glory

in their cages and sets them down on the bench. Then she runs back to clip me to my leash and we join the others. Mona is breathing hard as she sits next to Glory.

"This is so exciting!" says Mona.

Cars come in and out of the parking lot. Families push strollers along the path. A clump of people stands around a little ways off. I'm not sure what I'm missing. I've watched a bug crawl along the edge of a leaf, and it was more exciting than this. Then all of a sudden, *whoosh*. A great stream of water pounds up out of the ground.

Mona claps her hands. Glory flaps her wings and crows like a rooster. The water shoots up as high as a tree and then drifts off at the top like a feather. I can't take my eyes off it for a minute, but then I look away. Honestly, I'm a little embarrassed and I'll tell you why.

I never knew this, but now it's clear that even the land needs to pee sometimes. It happens to all of us, and I suppose it's no different for the land of Yellowstone.

But when I need to go, I don't like people staring at me. It makes me uncomfortable and, to tell the truth, it also makes it harder to go. There's a part of me that just locks up, and there I am with my leg in the air and nothing coming out.

So that's why I look away. Sure, I'm impressed. That's a lot of water. And I want to look. It just doesn't seem very polite.

∽

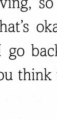

"That was worth the whole trip to Yellowstone!" Back in the car, Mona has the volume turned up on her jazzy music and is making a drum out of her steering wheel. "Wasn't that just so amazing?" She reaches over and scratches her favorite dog behind the ears. Mmm, nice.

I'm thinking that a nice scratching session could be amazing, but Mona is driving, so the scratching doesn't last very long. That's okay. I have something else on my mind. I go back to check on a certain white rat. "Did you think that was amazing, Heckles?"

He is chewing on a piece of cardboard and he looks at me, but he doesn't answer.

"Pretty cool, huh? All that gushing water soaring up to the sky like a giant rat tail?" I think I'm clever to say that part about the rat tail. Hector doesn't look so impressed. He sticks out his tongue and then digs himself under a lump of sawdust. I get the message that I haven't been forgiven.

"I'm sorry, Heckles," I say to the lump. There's no answer. I can tell I'm going to have to work at this before we can be friends again.

❦

When we pull into camp, guess who rushes out to meet us? Alexandra hardly waits for the car to stop. I'm in the front seat, but she unlatches the back door this time. "Aunt Mona, you were gone forever. Can I play with Hector? I'm gonna be Cinderella and I need a rat coachman."

All of a sudden I know just what I can do to show Hector that I'm a good friend. I know I'm going to be in deep trouble for this, but I've made up my mind. I jump in the backseat and I bark like crazy. I bark my head off.

Alexandra jumps back. That's the good part.

Mona yells at me. That's the bad part. "Lobo, no! Lobo, stop that." I knew she was going to yell at me. I knew my barking was going to disappoint her. Still, I have to do it. I bark some more, until Mona finally grabs my collar.

"Alexandra, honey, it's been a long day in the car for me and my family." Mona picks me up and gets out of the car. "Lobo is obviously grouchy and probably Hector is too. Maybe you'd better wait and play Cinderella another time."

Mona walks to the motor home. "For now I know that there is one cranky little fellow who has just earned himself a time-out." Mona steps up into the motor home and clips my leash to the armrest of a chair.

She talks more softly now, but her words cut deep. "I'm so disappointed in you, Lobo," she says. "You know you can't act like that with my niece. I hope you feel bad."

The door closes and it's just me. Alone. In time-out. And I do feel bad. I always feel bad when Mona is disappointed in me, even if it's not very wolfish of me.

But there's a tiny part of me that doesn't feel bad. I had to show Hector that I really meant it when I said I was sorry.

Later the door opens. Mona unclips me, picks me up, and cuddles me like she always does after time-out. Ooh, that feels good. She even forgets to clip me back up to my leash. On the way to the campfire, I see Hector in his cage on a little rug, but I can't catch his eye to see if we're friends yet.

Then comes the part when I have to make it up to Alexandra. Yuck. But I do what Mona wants. Mona holds me while I let Alexandra pet my head. I act all nice, and as a reward I get a beautiful necklace. Actually, it is a piece of yellow yarn with loops in it.

"You may wear the princess's golden chain." Alexandra ties it around my neck. I can tell that Mona thinks this is cute. I think it's going to get in my way. At least Mona makes sure it isn't tied too tightly. Then Alexandra goes to sit on her mother's lap.

Mona sits by the campfire with me on her lap, and we watch the sun go down. She pets me. She runs her fingers through my hair. She picks off the little eye boogers that end up all crusty and gross on my cheek. It feels so good.

There is a sleepy feeling going around the group. Then somebody mentions s'mores, and all of a sudden I get dropped on the ground.

I hate s'mores. They taste terrible, and they break apart and get all over the fingers of the people who love them. Then the fingers touch you and before you know it, the sticky goo is all over your fur.

Mona is crazy about them. So are Alexandra and her parents and her grandparents. For that matter, probably even Glory and Hector love s'mores.

That gives me an idea. Hector has *got* to love them. He loves everything sticky and gooey and crunchy. I prowl under the chairs. No one is watching. I sneak around and look for my chance, and then it happens. Just like they always do, someone drops a big chunk of s'more.

I can't believe I'm doing this, but before any-one can step on the s'more and make it even worse, I pick it up in my teeth. Yeegh! It's so gummy and sweet and covered with pine needles that I can hardly breathe while I take it over to Hector's cage. Plus I step on the princess's golden chain with every other step. But when I get there, Hector is drooling from the smell.

"I figured you wouldn't want to be left out." I drop it and use my tongue to feel around. Sure enough. Melted marshmallow all over my whiskers.

"Push it over here, closer." Hector's little hands

are stretching for it, but they can't quite reach. I nose it closer and get melted marshmallow on my nose.

Hector grabs the treat and hurries it into a corner of his cage. He's about to take a bite, but then he stops and looks at me.

"Um . . . thanks," he says.

"I'm sorry about tricking you in the car today," I say.

A drop of drool drips out of his mouth, but Hector puts his nose up to the wire of his cage. "Thanks for getting Alexandra to leave me alone in the car. I hope time-out wasn't too bad."

I shake my head.

Then he notices my new jewelry. "What's that around your neck? Some kind of new punishment?"

"No," I say. "Reward. I get to wear the princess's golden necklace for mending my bad ways."

"Nice," he says.

"No hard feelings?" I say.

"No hard feelings. Bump me." Hector sticks out his knuckles and we bump. "Mind if I dig in?" he says.

"Just don't save any for me," I say. "I hate that stuff."

Hector takes a big bite. Brown and white slime squishes out of the corners of his mouth. "Mmph or ghrassier glurb ah erff."

Yeah, that makes sense. I walk away because I don't want to watch that mess. Plus, I have to lick off the goo from my nose and whiskers. When I'm clean, I jump back into Mona's lap and she lets me stay. I curl up. Sleep is going to feel excellent.

Just then I remember that for the first time since we got to Yellowstone, I don't have my leash on, and I forgot to make a break for it and find my pack. Oh well. I'm too tired tonight anyway, and I'm sure I will get my chance tomorrow.

Yes, I'll make my move tomorrow for sure.

Freedom!

Two hands wake me up. Mona isn't usually such an early riser. She must need to take an early morning walk to sniff that fresh air. It sounds good to me. A good start to the day will help me forget the problems of yesterday. Good old Mona.

Then I get lifted up so that my legs are dangling. Have I mentioned how much wolf brothers hate having their legs dangled in the air? I struggle a little to remind Mona to hold me the way I like.

I look up. It isn't Mona. It's Alexandra again.

Never mind struggling. I consider a good sharp bite to just one of those little fingers. It would do so much good, but I remember what Glory said about family. I'm about to bark and let someone know I'm being kidnapped when Alexandra begins to speak.

"Are you lonely too?" she whispers.

Me? I look around for another human.

"Are you cold?"

I might be trembling a bit. But I'm not cold.

"Hector and Glory are cold too. And lonely."

They are? I have never heard of being lonely before breakfast. As I'm trying to figure out what this means, Alexandra unlatches Hector's cage, unhooks my chain, and puts me inside.

Imagine this. I have come to Yellowstone Park with the notion that I might be able to taste a bit of freedom. Instead I am being shoved into a cage that would make a prairie dog feel cramped.

My sleepiness drops away the minute my feet touch Hector's sawdust. Wet.

Glory is here too, and it doesn't look like she's enjoying the experience any more than I am.

She looks at me and I don't have to ask what

she's thinking. Just wait it out and it will be over sooner or later.

I tiptoe around trying to find a dry spot. But the little guy has made a mess of the place everywhere. I try to convince myself that Hector has somehow managed to spill his water. But the smell lets me know the truth of the matter, and the disgusting little black peanut things lying around are . . . not peanuts.

I try to keep my nose closed and breathe through my mouth.

Hector opens his eyes. He looks as if he can't quite figure out where he is.

Alexandra's face is pushed up close to the wire. If she could fit, I think she would crawl in with us.

Just then I hear footsteps coming from the back of the motor home. That's a good sign. Mona will put us back where we belong.

Alexandra hears it too.

"Uh-oh," she whispers. "Somebody's coming. We better get you outside before you get in trouble."

Me get in trouble? What did I do?

She picks up the cage, and the whole thing

bucks and heaves while she stands up. "Earth-quake," Hector moans. "Keep to the high ground."

I don't understand why this is important until I find myself at the bottom of the heap with a rat's foot in my ear and my face smashed into wet sawdust.

We all lurch and sway and knock into each other.

Even with a rat's foot in my ear, my sensitive

hearing can pick up sounds. I hear Alexandra unlatch the door of the motor home. She's making a clean getaway with her stolen treasure. Meanwhile, the treasure is getting airsick.

Then it happens. As she rushes down the motor home steps, the cage slips out of her hands. We flip through the air, clatter to the ground, and roll over two times. I might mention that none of us have on our seat belts. I might also mention that keeping my feet dry is not as important to me now as keeping the wet sawdust out of my ears, eyes, and mouth.

We tumble over each other in a mash of feathers, fur, wet sawdust, and little black peanuts that aren't actually peanuts.

I lift my head, shake my ears, and see that the door of the cage has popped open in the crash.

"Make a break for it!" Hector yells.

He doesn't need to say it twice. I break for freedom and over my head I feel a rush of feathers.

"Que libertad!" Even Glory isn't going to pass up this chance. She might like sitting around in a cage, but not *that* cage.

"Free! Free!" squeaks Hector. I see flashes of white as he scuttles through the dust of the campsite, over the road, and into the tall grass on the other side. For a short-legged guy he is moving awfully fast.

"Come back, come back," Alexandra screeches. "I'll get in trouble if you don't come back."

If escaping her clutches isn't enough motivation, she has just put the gravy on the dog biscuit. I, for one, am going to do my part to make sure she gets in as much trouble as possible.

I dash after Hector through the dust and over the road. I dodge around a root.

"Ulp." My legs fly out from under me. I land with a thud in a puff of dust. "Save yourselves," I choke. "They've got me."

Behind us, Alexandra gives a little scream of joy.

Suddenly Hector is back at my side. "Get up, you lazy mutt. Your ancestors are waiting for you and you'll never find them lying on your back."

Good advice. I scramble up. Take one step. Hit the dirt again.

"It's the princess necklace," shouts Glory from the nearest tree. "It's caught."

I crane my neck and see she's right. The loop in the end of my golden princess necklace has hooked the root, and I'm stuck fast.

Thud. Thud.

Alexandra's footsteps.

I moan and close my eyes.

Then I feel Hector at my neck and hear the *snick, snick* of his yellow teeth. The yarn falls from my neck and lies in pieces in the dust.

"Run," he says. "Hurry up. Go make us proud, wolfy junior."

I feel rather than see Alexandra's hands reaching. I scramble up, teeter a moment, then run. Just behind me comes the mighty thump and wail of girl falling into dust.

I streak for the road following Hector's fast feet.

"Don't go too far." Glory flaps over my head. "Hector, stay out of sight. Your white fur is like a flag calling every predator in the park. And behave yourself with the ladies."

I find my wolf legs and race by Hector. "Find a hole and run down it," I shout over my shoulder. "And thanks."

"You don't have to tell me twice," squeals Hector. "Where's the rodent hangout around this place? Because here comes the party man." He disappears into a bush and doesn't come out the other side.

I run with Glory above me until I can see we're safe. She lands on the branch of a tree and I stop.

"Thanks for your help back there," I say.

"Stay right here with me." She tips her head to one side. "You're not as big as you think you are."

"Stay here?" I say. "I can't. This is my chance for the wild life. You should run for it too. Or fly for it."

"Oh, no." She shakes all her feathers, and little bits of sawdust fly off. "I'm a city girl. I don't need any of that kind of trouble. I'm just going to hang around here for a while and play it safe. You should too."

"Thanks, Glory." I stare up. "After I find my pack, I'm sure we won't meet up again, but you've been a great friend."

She looks sad. "Lobo, listen to my advice just this one time. Go and take a peek around if you have to, but stay out of sight. Get this wild thing out of your system and come right back. It's too dangerous out there, Lobo. It's no place for a pup like you."

I grin. "Don't worry about me. I'll be fine. Think about yourself for once. You can get back to the wild life of your childhood."

She snorts. "I'm going right back to my cage just as soon as the little kidnapper gets what she deserves, and the coast is clear." Then she fluffs her feathers and tucks her neck down into her shoulders. "It's cold out here. I just hope Mona wakes up soon."

"Well, bye then." I can't wait to be on my way. I head down a track in the direction I heard the howls coming from last night.

My Destiny

After a little bit of sniffing, I find a trail through the brush. It has footprints and droppings and all the stuff a wild trail should have, including dust.

I'm so happy, I pick up one of my hind feet and skip down the path on three wheels. Then I remember that wolves probably don't do too much skipping.

Just in case someone is watching, I decide it's time to start fitting in. Skipping will never do for an alpha wolf. But neither will my usual run. It's more like a skitter.

Somewhere down the line I got into this bad habit of skittering. Since I never had a true wolf role model, there was no one to correct me or show me how to run properly. I was going to have to figure this one out on my own.

Loping, I think. *That's how wolves run.* Legs high, feet together and kind of bouncy. First the front end bounces up and then the back end. Loping is like a horse galloping, but happier.

I'm going to tell you right now, loping isn't as easy as it might appear. It takes a little while to get the hang of a good lope. In fact, a lope might be the sort of thing that works better on a long-legged animal. Not that my legs are short. A little undersized, maybe.

A few steps down the trail, I think I'm getting the hang of it. My paws are flopping around like the big dogs I watch back in the city. I'm leaping forward with each powerful thrust of my hind legs, and I can feel my tail flowing out behind me.

Then one of my front paws forgets to flop forward, and I stumble. I pretty near sprain an ankle and definitely eat some Yellowstone trail dirt. It tastes about as bad as you might think. Dusty with a strong aroma of dirt. And since this is a foot trail, it has just a hint of bottom-of-foot flavor.

Now, this is an experience I don't want to repeat, so I decide to take a break from loping and go back to skittering—temporarily.

The sun is just beginning to come up. The air is fresh and clean. Each puff of breeze brings a whiff of smells that are wild and new.

But something is missing. I try to think what it is. My dream is coming true but somehow something feels wrong.

Mona.

I stop. What will Mona think when she sees I've run off? A very bad feeling comes into my tummy, and for the first time in my life it isn't hunger. What about Mona, who brought me home when I was just a puppy and made me feel safe? Who will protect her on road trips? Who will look at photo albums with her and go for walks in the park?

In my mind I see Mona wandering all over Yellowstone calling my name.

I almost turn around right there and run back.

Almost.

Then I come to my senses. What am I thinking? I have a wolf family out there. Any dog with any pride at all takes his very first chance to join the wild pack and never looks back. He lives to hunt with the big boys. Mona can get a cat if she wants something that sleeps all day and never thinks about his wild side.

I go back to skittering and put all thoughts of Mona right out of my head.

After a while the trail ends at a big grassy meadow. There are smells of all sorts here. Most noses, of course, wouldn't be able to tell them apart.

I can tell that deer have used this meadow. My nose is assisted by the fact that there are piles of little black marbles lying all around that are too big for rabbit . . . marbles.

I lope . . . that is to say, I half skitter, half lope around the edge of the grassy meadow. I am looking and smelling for something. Deer smells are just fine when you're looking for a deer. But I'm after a different smell.

When I find it, the hairs on the back of my neck stand up.

I sniff the bush again. Yes! All wolves and their

descendents leave their calling cards on bushes. Now it's my turn to add my calling card to the stack.

Leaving a calling card is something dogs practice every day of their lives. Especially boy dogs. It's not an easy thing to explain. An animal without my mental toughness would probably get embarrassed by this explanation, but not me.

First, you lift up your leg. It doesn't matter which leg, exactly, but it should definitely be a back leg. Lift it up high, because the next part could get a little messy if you aren't careful.

Now balance, wait for it, and if everything is operating correctly, pretty soon you'll feel something like a tickle. Or maybe it's more like an itch. No, it's not a tickle or an itch, but it *is* a feeling. (I know this is getting complicated, but stay with me because we're almost done.)

Then the last thing is to check behind yourself to make sure you aimed correctly. That's it! This whole process leaves you feeling proud and puts an extra bounce in your lope. Everyone should try it. Ask any wolf or his relatives.

I lift my leg, leave my calling card—very, very

expertly, by the way—and then lope off to find myself a place to wait.

I know from the fresh smell of the calling cards that wolves like to come to this meadow often, and I am sure that they will be back soon. I don't want to scare off any potential prey, so I decide to find a hiding place.

There's a clump of tall grass on a high bank that overlooks the meadow. I crawl inside the clump and wait for my brothers.

A Life-and-Death Matter

I lie perfectly still. Completely camouflaged. Unseen. A top predator at his most dangerous. Totally invisible.

Then a fly lands on my ear. It tickles. I do not stir. A top predator does not break his cover for any reason short of life and death. The fly circles the edge of my ear and tickles some more. I do not move a muscle.

The fly takes a sightseeing adventure—southbound. It's walking on the inside of my ear! The tickle curls my paws, but otherwise I remain still as a statue. It turns out this fellow has a special move saved up for me. It's called the go-deep-and-then-buzz-as-loud-as-you-can move.

I jump about four feet in the air and hit the ground running, shaking my head as hard as I can. My ear has decided this is a life-and-death matter.

When I am sure the bug has taken his game somewhere else, I hop back into my hiding place. If any wary prey has seen that display of strength and agility, they will be long gone. All the rodents and vermin who happened to be watching at that moment are shivering at the bottoms of their holes.

The thought of vermin makes me think about Hector and the way he helped me get away from Alexandra. I hope he is meeting girl rats, and that at least one of them doesn't find him as ugly or disgusting as I do.

He's fine, I tell myself. He is probably having a party.

But what if the other rats take a disliking to that strange white fur and kick him out? Then where will he go? He can't hide. At night he practically glows. An owl or a weasel would make short work of him.

What? Is it possible I'm worried about Hector? Never in a million dog years did I think I would worry about that little pest. But here I am fretting about him.

Maybe Glory is watching out for him. It would be just like her to spend her free days checking up on the little guy instead of testing the wild winds of Yellowstone. I think of her racing down a canyon on wings that feel young and quick again.

If I wasn't such a cold-blooded predator, I would say that I miss them both. I would say that I am going soft and that I care about those two unfortunate critters. But a cold-blooded predator has no time for such tender feelings. He thinks of one thing only—survival for himself and for the pack.

I lie very still in my hiding place and remind myself over and over that my pack is out there somewhere. They will bound over to me when they see me. Their heads will be up, ready to welcome the newest hunter into their group. The wolf leader will lick my nose and I will lick his and then we will sniff each other.

We will sniff noses, and we will sniff necks and shoulders. Sniffing is a big deal in the dog world. Then we will move down and sniff sides and back legs. And then will come the big finish of the sniffing business, where we will sniff... Well, never mind that part. If you're not a dog or a wolf, you might not understand. The important thing is that we will sniff each other and then we will hunt.

While I am running through all that sniffing in my mind, the sun is getting hotter and hotter. My hiding place is getting more and more uncomfortable. Grass and sticks can poke the soft underbelly of even the most ferocious top predator. There is another thing that's getting uncomfortable.

My stomach.

I start thinking about dog food. Delicious, crunchy, perfectly sized dog food and a cool bowl of water right next to the food. "No," I whisper sternly. A wolf, even a wolf in training, does not crave dog food. He does not wish for crisp, duck-flavored Nibbles and Nuggets, perfectly identical, tested for taste on millions of dogs ... *Stop it*, I tell myself.

Instead, I work over my introduction lines.

"Howdy, folks." I'm pleased with how deep and smooth my voice sounds in my mind. "Do you reckon you could use another really wild, really brave hunting partner?" I call that my bold Western approach. Always effective.

Or I could say, "Jumping jackrabbits. I was just about to go out on another one of my fantastically successful hunting trips. Want to come along?" I call that my surprised-but-happy-to-meet-you approach.

Or I could impress them with the city-dog-meets-country-cousin approach. "Hot dog in hamburger heaven. Haven't I seen you before?"

A loping sound makes me lift my head, and at the far edge of the meadow I see them.

Wolves!

The Hunt

All my fancy introductions fly out of my head. I won't deny it. I am thrilled. I am so thrilled that my feet are shaking, and my shaky feet make my legs shake, which makes my whole body shake.

This is the most exciting moment of my life. I am maybe just a touch overwhelmed at the sight of the greatest hunters in the world.

I watch them glide into the meadow grass that reaches almost up to their bellies. I stay perfectly still. A fly could land on my eyeball, jump into my ear, walk across my brain and out the other side, and I would not make a sound.

The wolves are beautiful and frightening. They are just as amazing as I thought they would be, only more so.

At first I think they are just there for a little romp in the grass. But the lead wolf changes direction suddenly and starts sniffing this way and that.

The other wolves join in on either side. They move as if they are one wolf.

I know what they are doing. Something is hiding for its life in the tall grass. The hunt is on.

Suddenly they leap into action. The lead wolf charges forward with the other two close beside. I can't see what they're pursuing, but I know a hunt when I see it. Whenever the prey darts left, the wolf on the left cuts it off.

They are powerful and fast.

There is no escape.

Then the animal, the prey, jumps into the air for a second, and I see what they are chasing. It's a rabbit. A brown fellow with a white tail. He has tried everything else to escape, and now he is leaping. But it's too late. As soon as he lands, the teeth are just inches away.

My heart is knocking on my ribs. I know that

the end is near for the rabbit. To my horror, I realize that I'm rooting for the little guy to get away.

I've never been so shocked in all my life. What sort of wolf brother ever cheers for the rabbit?

I stand frozen. The chase stops short. The lead wolf dips his head in the grass and jerks his head back and forth. I can't see it but I imagine the quick bite. And then the stillness. The three hunters lift their heads and look around while they catch their breath.

Yellow eyes. Yellow eyes boring into anything that moves. If you get locked onto by a pair of those eyes, you stay looked at. That's what happened to the rabbit.

That little guy never had a chance. It wasn't exactly a fair fight. He was seven times smaller than even one wolf. And there were three of them.

For a second, I think about walking out there and telling them to pick on someone their own size. I think about marching right out and staring them down. And then it hits me. I am about the same size as the rabbit they are about to snack on.

I crouch in the grass. I decide to stay right where I am. Only a little bit lower down.

"Get it over with," I whisper.

But they still don't eat that poor rabbit. Instead they lift their noses in the air, throw their heads back and forth, and sniff really hard. Something has caught their attention. Something that seems mighty interesting.

I settle myself down for another show. I promise myself that this time I won't root for the prey. It's all about survival, I tell myself. You can't be softhearted when you're the top predator.

"Okay, brother wolves. Go git him," I whisper.

That's when I realize that the wind has shifted. It's blowing from behind me, over my back, and down onto the meadow.

My brother wolves are walking my way.

Something is so interesting to them that they have left that dead rabbit where it lies in the grass.

They stroll over to a certain bush, and I suddenly wish I had not left my calling card right where any old top predator can find it and trace the scent another twenty feet over.

The trembling in my feet isn't excitement this time.

I wish I'd stayed with Mona.

I wish I'd listened to Glory.

I think about making a break for it. I think about how quickly I left Alexandra in the dust.

Then I think about how those wolves ran down a lightning-fast rabbit with all of its twisting and turning tricks.

No matter if I choose to run or just stay in my shivery clump of grass, it looks as if I have only a minute or two left to live.

I'm doomed.

Brother Rat

The wolves don't move a blade of grass when they take a step. They are in no hurry.

I can see every whisker now, every silver hair among the gold and brown and black. They are beautiful. They are strong and confident.

And they are going to eat me.

The sun is burning hot on the top of my head, and I think about how I have seen my last sunset.

Just when it seems as if it can't get any worse, it does.

A flash of white catches my eye. A fat little

rodent waddles his way down the dry, dusty bank to the meadow just behind the wolves. He must not have seen the wolves. Rats can't see very well. He is looking at that nice, green meadow grass.

I can just imagine what he's thinking. He's thinking about all the hiding places and girl rats who would definitely make a home in such a beautiful place.

Unfortunately, I'm not the only one who sees him.

The wolves turn. They don't miss a thing. They have heard his little scurrying footsteps. At first they just stare as if they can't believe their eyes. It's possible that tasty rodents in Yellowstone Park don't often waddle by dressed in an easy-to-spot white outfit, all fattened up and ready to eat.

They don't just stand and stare for long. You don't become a top predator by standing around and staring when your midday snack strolls by.

The wolves turn their backs on me. I think about jumping up right then and hightailing it out of there. But my legs won't move.

The rat stops in his tracks. He sees the trouble he is in too late.

You might think I'm thrilled to have the wolves get interested in someone else. But I am not thrilled at all. I know, for sure, that it is my brother rat in the dirt.

As I watch, the wolves surround Hector. I can see his face clearly now. It is a face I have seen every morning of my life.

He crouches down as low as he can go in the dust and shows his yellow teeth. I've always thought those teeth were creepy, but these wolves don't seem too impressed. In fact, the wolves seem to be grinning.

One of them reaches out a paw and flips Hector over. Another one grabs him in his teeth and tosses him spinning in the air.

They are playing with him.

It's too much for me to watch. I can't do it. My legs stand up on their own. I take a step. My brain screams at me to run in the opposite direction. But my legs run me right toward those wolves.

Unbelievably, I bark at them.

I reach right down to the biggest, fiercest part of me and woof with all the power I can muster.

Okay, I admit it. I yap. I yip and yap, and I give it everything I have.

They aren't going to gobble down my friend without a fight. These top predators will learn what it's like to face down the baddest pet-store Chihuahua the world has ever seen.

Okay, I'll admit that my loudest and angriest barking has never caused anyone to run away in fear. Or even to back away slowly.

But I'm hoping that just this once the wolves will tuck their tails and run.

They don't.

They also don't wag their tails and walk up to me in a friendly, sniffing sort of way.

Instead they all pull their lips over their teeth and snarl. There is no sound in the universe as frightening as the snarl of a wild wolf.

Ice tingles spread down my legs. But I'm not going to stop barking. Okay, yapping.

I yap like I've never yapped before. I yap as if twenty burglars have broken into Mona's apartment. I yap as if a hundred buffalo have gotten loose in Central Park, and it's up to me to move them along. I yap as if it were my last yap—which I figure it probably is. Then I yap some more.

And for just a moment, it seems to confuse the wolves. They look at me as if this is something they might need to take a minute to figure out. Before they eat it.

I see Hector gather himself off the ground where he landed. He begins to sneak a few steps closer to the meadow. Then he makes a dash for it and disappears into the long grass. I hope there's a hole somewhere close by.

The wolves don't notice. In a stiff-legged way, they begin to move in my direction. I stop yapping. There are no snarls now. Heads low and ears forward, the pack is done figuring or being confused or surprised.

They are hunting.

It's all over.

Crazy Bird

I stop barking. My thoughts echo inside my head. No more road trips in Mona's sporty car. No more exercise runs around her apartment. No more crunchy doggy chow Nibbles and Nuggets all the same size.

Step by step the wolves close in on me. There is no hurry, no doubt in those six yellow eyes about how this is going to end. I have eaten my last doggy biscuit. I have felt the last rush of wind in my ears out of a car window. I have enjoyed my last tummy party.

I also think I have seen the last surprise of the day.

I'm wrong.

A flash of green suddenly falls out of the sky in between me and the wolves.

The wolves stop their stalking. We all stare at this strange fluttering collection of bright green leaves. It's flopping around on the ground in a circle.

As I watch, it flops under the feet of the wolves and makes them jump back. They sniff at it and get a snoot full of dust for their trouble.

It flops over to me.

I sniff at it—and catch sight of an eyeball.

"Split!" whispers the collection of leaves with an eyeball. "Run!" Then in a louder voice it moans, "Oooh, my stomach. I think I'm dying."

That is no collection of leaves. That is a bird. My powerful reasoning ability tells me this.

"Call a doctor," it screeches.

A poor diseased bird. An unfortunate traveling parrot that has been blown off course and has chosen the exact wrong spot to get sick.

I sniff again at the bird and get punched in the

nose by a wing for my trouble. "Go home, you walnut-headed dingbat," it whispers.

Huh? A sick bird that still has enough pep in it to be insulting? I back up a step to put a little distance between me and this crazy thing with the spicy tongue and the good, strong left hook. The sick bird flops and flutters back over to the wolves, who seem more and more interested.

As I stare, the bird flaps helplessly downhill toward the meadow. The wolves cautiously follow.

"*Que stupido!*" the doomed bird squawks. "Get out of here, you bug-eyed mutt!"

Now, most bug-eyed mutts wouldn't know what to do in that situation. Most bug-eyed mutts would have no idea what their next move should be. But I have no such confusion.

I charge out of there as if I'm on fire. I tuck tail and run just as hard as I can in the direction of Mona and the motor home and darling Alexandra.

I don't lope. I scamper. Honestly, I'm not concerned about how I'm moving. I'm just dashing and dodging in a way that gets me gone from that meadow as fast as possible.

There is no thundering of feet behind me. There is no hot breath on my hindquarters, no snapping of teeth. It doesn't matter. I keep dashing.

There's one thing wolves don't know about Chihuahuas. Parrots don't know this either. Or rats. Chihuahuas don't even know this about Chihuahuas. If there are wolves behind them, they can move very fast!

A Glorious Escape

Safety. Shelter. My poor brain whispers to me over and over. Mona. Humans. Motor homes with big butts and cars with the windows rolled up. It all seems wonderful to me at the moment. I'm moving faster than a New York taxi on a day with no traffic.

I hope Glory is waiting back at camp.

Glory?

I stop running. In a Chihuahua-sized cloud of dust, I pull up short. My brain starts an argument with my legs. My legs want to keep going. They are just trying to do their job, I suppose, and they won't stop dancing around. But my brain has cleared in a snap.

Que stupido! Que problema! I know that voice. I know that phony Spanish accent. That is no stranger in green feathers behind me. The truest, bravest friend I have is about to be torn apart by big and unforgiving teeth. And all because she got sick in the wrong place at the wrong time.

I can't let it happen.

I have to go back. I have to try and save her. But how did Glory get sick so quickly? When we left camp, she was fine.

I turn around. I get those legs moving the other way.

Suddenly, something dive-bombs me from above. A large, dog-eating bird of prey swoops down on me, screaming and aiming its giant beak at my eyes.

I fling myself on the ground as low as I can. But I know it isn't going to do any good. I'm not going to be able to rescue anybody. I am about to be carried away and fed piece by piece to young, hungry eagle babies.

To escape from wolves and end up as eagle burger is the worst thing that I can think of. I crouch and wait for the claws to seize my body and lift me into the air.

"Run, you fool!" The screeching turns to words—words in a fabulous, dear, familiar voice. "They're right behind you!"

My legs push off. My toes dig in. No scrabbling and slipping over hardwood floors. My ears fly back, and I glue my eyes to the green flier ahead of me. I never look back. In a short time I can see the road. I can smell the hot dogs and spicy mustard from the campers. *Don't stop. Don't even slow down*, I tell my legs.

I dash. I streak. I burn through the grass.

Once on the other side of that road, I know I'm safe. Glory flutters down and I leap up to meet her. We roll over each other on the ground laughing and celebrating like wild things.

"How did you get away?" I ask Glory when I'm too tired to jump and celebrate anymore. "And how did you get well so fast?"

She falls to the ground in a heap of feathers. "Call the doctor!" she moans.

"Oh, Glory!" I say. "How did you know the perfect thing to do?"

Glory picks herself up off the ground and shakes off the dust. "You don't get to be as old as I am without tucking a few tricks under your wing. If you pretend to be sick and helpless enough, predators don't think they have to rush in for the kill, and you can distract them."

Wow!

Glory is smarter than us all. For a moment I wonder what she would do if I were to give her a big, wet, slobbery kiss. "Those aren't just tricks. Those are wild tricks, Glory," I tell her. "Those are jungle-bird, fly-in-your-face, don't-even-think-about-sticking-me-in-a-cage tricks."

"Well, let's not get carried away." Glory shakes the dust off her feathers. "I like my cage just fine and I don't need any extra excitement."

We start walking toward the motor home. Glory has a long, striding, side-to-side, swing-your-tail-back-and-forth sort of walk I have never seen before.

Then I stop. "Glory," I say quietly, "no one made you come save me. You could have just let me run

off on my own and let me get snapped up in the wilderness. It would have served me right."

Glory gives her feathers a shake. "Oh, I would have to agree with you. It definitely would have served you right. I probably should have."

She chuckles. "But what a glorious escape we had. And my goodness, you were a little blur. *Que rapido.* I don't know where it came from, but I do believe there is a bit of wild-wolf speed in those little legs of yours."

A few moments later, we reach the motor home. From the way Glory hunkers down as she creeps toward the steps, I know we are thinking the same thing. *Alexandra could be waiting. Make a quiet entrance.* But it isn't meant to be.

We hear a screech. "Glory and Lobo came home!" That's Alexandra. I brace myself for the attack. But it never comes.

Because Mona beats her to it.

She scoops both Glory and me up in her arms before Alexandra can get to us, and twirls around and hugs us. I even get a kiss on the nose.

Truthfully, I don't mind. Maybe I even like it.

When she is finally done hugging and kissing us, she puts us in the motor home.

Alexandra tries to get past, but Mona playfully grabs the monster, gives her a noogie, and tells her that we have had enough loving to last us for a while.

I have to agree.

Quite a while.

The door closes. The footsteps and whining noises fade, and for a long moment I listen to the quiet and look around. Glory's cage has been shined up and cleaned. My pillow has been brushed.

Wow. We came so close to leaving Mona all alone.

I glance inside Hector's cage. Seeing it empty makes me sad. Someone has cleaned it out and put in fresh sawdust.

I wander over and sniff the bars up and down. "He'll never come back," I say.

"True. And thanks to you, he's not causing indigestion, rolling around in some wolf stomach." Glory flutters up to her cage and climbs in. "One question. What on earth made you turn around and head back toward that meadow?"

"When I figured out it was you who was sick . . . even though you weren't really—I had to go back for you."

Glory shakes her head. "You are brave," she says, "and a good friend."

I make a few circles.

She turns around and pokes her head out. "Now, enjoy your peace and quiet. I know I will."

I settle down on my own beloved pillow and try to enjoy the quiet.

But the quiet feels all wrong. "Actually, I kind of miss him," I say. "I wish I could tell him that."

Glory cracks open a few seeds. "I miss him too. Although heaven knows I won't miss all the squabbling and fighting around here."

"He's probably out there with a girl rat right now," I say. "He'll never give us another thought."

I hop up on the seat and looked out the window.

Stars are beginning to shine through.

I close my eyes.

"Lobo," Glory says softly. I look up. "I'm sorry your lifelong dream of finding your pack wasn't meant to be."

My Pack

It's true. If there was ever a time to feel sorry for myself, this is it.

I feel mixed up or dizzy or sick. I feel . . . I don't know what I feel.

Tired. That's one thing I feel.

Maybe after I get some rest I'll know what I'm feeling.

I close my eyes again and just start to doze when a happy scream from outside makes my ears shoot straight up. I leap to my feet and run in circles.

There are a few more shouts and then the door of the motor home bursts open. Mona hurries in and slides a fat little white rodent into his cage.

"Heckles?" I leap for joy and circle and bark and bark. Okay, I yap. I can't help it. I'm so happy.

"Thank goodness my family is all safe tonight," Mona says. "I don't know how I could go back to the city without you guys. Sweet dreams, everyone." She closes the motor home door.

I run up to the cage. "You came back. I can't believe you came back!"

"What a day." Hector flops down in a corner. "And what a night."

"Did you find a girl rat?"

"There was a girl rat on the other side of every dark tunnel," he says. "Those country girls love a party rat, let me tell you." He wiggles his toes.

"Then why did you ever come home?" I ask.

"Did I tell you it was dark? That's exactly the problem. It's dark down in those underground rat holes. I'm not used to creeping around in tight places." He rolls over and comes up to the side of his cage. "Especially if you happen to be carrying around a few extra love handles." Hector pinches

129

the extra fat on his tummy. "You can't even turn around in some of those rat highways. It's one-way traffic all day, every day, for a skinny country rat. But for a fat city rat, it's no-way traffic."

"So that's why you thought it was a good idea to hop out of your nice, safe hole and go strolling around in broad daylight," Glory says.

"Hey, you were right." Hector sighs. "No question about that. The minute you poke your head out for fresh air, it's nothing but teeth and claws and sharp beaks. Especially if you're a plump, tasty, good-looking fellow like me." He fluffs up some sawdust and flops back down.

I lie on my pillow and listen to the peaceful night noises of crickets and frogs. "Heckles . . . I mean Hector, I'm glad you came back," I say softly.

There is no answer, and I think the little guy must have fallen asleep. Then he coughs. "First of all," he says, "call me Heckles. I can't deal with any more surprises tonight. Second of all, I did a little thinking out there and decided I'm not going to meet anyone out there as good as you and the bird, who were both going to face down the biggest teeth on the continent just to save my smelly old self."

I sit up and look at him.

His tail gives a little twitch.

"And last of all, somebody has to make sure Glory doesn't sleep the days away with too much peace and quiet."

"Oh, for goodness' sake," says Glory. "Somebody put a towel over my cage and let me have some rest!"

Hector winks at me.

I put my head on my paws. The night is quiet for the moment. Then from far off comes a long, high, lonely howl. I hear Glory stir in her cage, and Hector and I sit up.

"Back to sleep," says Glory. "Just a family calling to itself. Everybody needs a family."

"The trick is to make sure someone else's family doesn't eat yours," says Hector.

I turn two and a half times and lie down. The sounds of the room settle all around me like the blankets Mona used to tuck me into when I was a lonely puppy. Heckles scratches himself, and his sawdust rustles as he tries to get more comfortable. Glory makes her feather-fluffing sounds and then grows quiet again.

"Glory," I say. I wait. I'm not sure anyone is listening. Then I decide to say it anyway. "You were wrong about one thing. I did find my pack in Yellowstone Park. I just didn't look for it in the right place. My pack lives in a place with air-conditioning, pizza, bright streetlights, and flavors from all over the world."

No one answers, but I don't care.

I know that starting tonight, I'm working on a whole new favorite dream. Somewhere under the dark trees, a pack is gathering together. They might be sniffing each other and getting ready for their family run. But I'm dreaming of my big, bold city home together with my own brave pack—Glory, Heckles, Mona, and me.

Catch the next

ANIMAL TALES

Here's a sneak peek at

Angus MacMouse
Brings Down the House

Minnie McGraw was reaching the end of her aria when she looked down and saw Angus standing quietly in the middle of the stage. Her face twisted in horror. She did not scream exactly, but her famous soprano voice kept getting higher, and higher, and *higher,* until she hit a note that no human being had ever hit before. A crackling noise came from the ceiling of the opera house, and every eye turned to look at the enormous crystal chandelier that hung over their heads. The orchestra stopped playing. The audience gasped. Then they heard a tinkling sound as thousands of crystals shattered and fell to the floor like glittering rain.

Some people cowered and screamed. Others clapped and cheered. Some yelled, "Bravo! Bravo!"

Minnie McGraw nearly fainted. She collapsed on the stage and began fanning herself.

Angus was confused and frightened. Had he done something wrong? As the audience rushed to leave, the huge velvet curtain came down with a thud. Everyone onstage gathered around him. They all looked very upset.

"Aach! It's a rat!"

"Oh, he's horrible. Filthy creature!"

"Look at those beady eyes."

"And that ugly tail."

"He ruined the opera!"

"Troublemaker!"

"Ne'er-do-well!"

Through the angry crowd a sweet voice called, "Wait! Don't hurt him!"